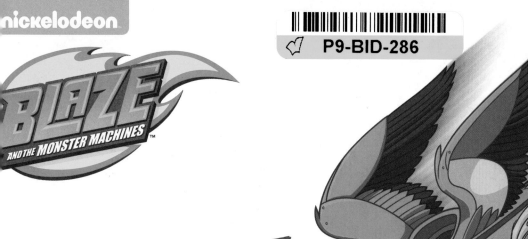

Adapted by Mary Tillworth

Based on the teleplay "Falcon Quest" by Gabe Pulliam and Halcyon Person

Illustrated by Dave Aikins

A Random House PICTUREBACK® Book

Random House  New York

© 2017 Viacom International Inc. All rights reserved. Published in the United States by Random House Children's Books, a division of Penguin Random House LLC, 1745 Broadway, New York, NY 10019, and in Canada by Penguin Random House Canada Limited, Toronto. Pictureback, Random House, and the Random House colophon are registered trademarks of Penguin Random House LLC. Nickelodeon, Nick Jr., Blaze and the Monster Machines, and all related titles, logos, and characters are trademarks of Viacom International Inc.

randomhousekids.com

ISBN 978-1-5247-6529-3

T#: 525946

Printed in the United States of America

10 9 8 7 6 5 4 3 2 1

One sunny morning, Blaze and his friends were zooming across Animal Island when suddenly, three shadows swooped overhead.

"Those are falcons!" cried Blaze.

Gabby watched them in awe. "They're so fast!"

AJ nodded. "Falcons are the fastest animals in the whole world!"

The falcons swooped down and landed next to Blaze.

One of the falcons winced. "Ow!" she said. "I think there's something wrong with my wing."

"I see the problem," Gabby said. "There's a thorn stuck in it!" She knew just what to do.

Gabby carefully pulled out the thorn.

"Thanks! That's much better." The falcon flexed her wing. "Good thing, too. I've gotta be fast for the Super Sky Race!"

AJ wanted to know more about the race, so he looked it up on his monitor. The Super Sky Race took place on an awesome course in the sky—with floating rings, loop-the-loops, and cloud tunnels!

"That looks amazing!" said Blaze.

Blaze sighed as he watched his falcon friends take off. "Wouldn't it be great if we could be in that sky race, too?"

Just then, Blaze heard a sharp laugh overhead. "As if you could be in the race. You can't even fly!" said a large falcon as he skidded down next to Blaze. "The name's Thunderwing. And I've got something you'll never have—wings! With these beauties, I'm gonna win the Super Sky Race!"

Thunderwing sneered as he flew away, chanting his own name.
"I know how we can fly in the Super Sky Race," said Blaze.
"Let's build our own wings! First we'll make tail feathers so I can
steer. Then I'll need strong talons for grabbing things. Finally, the
most important part: the wings so I can fly!"

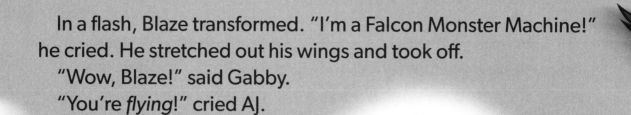

In a flash, Blaze transformed. "I'm a Falcon Monster Machine!" he cried. He stretched out his wings and took off.
"Wow, Blaze!" said Gabby.
"You're *flying*!" cried AJ.

Blaze swooped down. "Hop on!" he told Gabby and AJ. "We've got to hurry and get to that starting line!" "Super Sky Race, here we come!" yelled Gabby.

Gabby pointed to a floating arrow. "Check it out—there's a sign for the race!"

As they followed the arrow, dark storm clouds closed in around them, and they heard loud claps of thunder.

"Gaskets!" Blaze ducked when the wind started to hurl leaves and branches his way.

"We've got to get out of this storm, or we'll never get to the race!" said Gabby.

"Look, down there!" shouted AJ, pointing to a hole in the clouds. "Falcons fly fastest when they dive!" he told Blaze.

"With their aerodynamic shape, they can dive at speeds of up to one hundred meters per second," said Gabby.

Blaze folded his wings. "Here I *goooo*!" He plummeted toward the opening and burst through the storm—just in time!

As they soared across the sky, the friends saw another floating arrow.
"To get to the race, we need to fly through that tunnel," said Blaze.
"Hang on, everyone!"

Blaze flew into the tunnel. In the darkness, creepy plants wriggled out of the cracks. They reached for Blaze, trying to pinch him!

"They're growing everywhere," said Gabby. "Even out of the ceiling!"

"How are we going to get past them all?" asked AJ.

"I know! Let's steer around them with my tail feathers!" Blaze suggested.
"When falcons move their tail feathers, it changes how the air moves around them," Gabby explained. "And that lets them steer up and down!"
Using his tail feathers, Blaze carefully navigated around the pinching plants.

The friends flew out of the tunnel and into the sunlight.

"So long, pinching plants!" AJ laughed.

"Next stop: the Super Sky Race!" called Blaze as he soared through the air.

Gabby spotted one more floating arrow. "The starting line is at the top of this mountain!"

"We're almost there. Falcon, *flyyyy*!" cried Blaze.

As they rose higher and higher, the air got colder and colder. Then gigantic ice crystals broke from the side of the mountain and tumbled toward Blaze!

"There's only one way to get past falling ice crystals." Blaze snatched one. "I've got to crush them with my falcon talons!" *CRUNCH!*

"Falcons have strong talons for grabbing food when they're hunting," said AJ.

"With talons like that, Blaze could crush those ice crystals *before* they crash into us!" said Gabby.

Blaze sped up the mountain, crushing crystals left and right.

At the top of the mountain, Blaze saw his falcon friends. He had made it to the Super Sky Race!

"Hey, Blaze—you gonna race with us?" asked one of the falcons. Blaze nodded. "You bet I am!"

Thunderwing swooped down. "Aren't you forgetting something? You can't race, because you can't fly!"

Blaze extended his mighty falcon wings. "Oh, yes I can!" He joined his friends at the starting line.

"All right, racers!" called the announcer. "On your marks, get set . . . *fly!*"

Blaze took off, soaring easily through the race course.
"Nice flyin', dude!" called one of his falcon friends.
"You've got this!" cried another as Blaze took the lead.

But Thunderwing was determined to win—even if it meant cheating! He knocked into some floating rings so they would slam into Blaze. The Falcon Monster Machine spiraled out of control! "Ha, ha!" cackled Thunderwing, surging ahead.

"We can still beat him. I just need Blazing Speed!" Blaze flapped his wings faster and faster, until they glowed with energy. "Let's *blaaaze*!" he shouted.

Blaze zipped through cloud tunnels and loop-the-loops, crossing the finish line just ahead of Thunderwing!

"Falcon Blaze has done it! He's won the Super Sky Race!" cried the announcer.

"You were great out there!" cheered Blaze's friends.
Just then, Thunderwing flew over. Blaze looked at him nervously.
Thunderwing grinned. "Man, you really are an amazing flyer!"
Blaze gave him a high tire. "Thanks!"